KINGFISHER TREASURIES

A *wealth of stories to share!*

Ideal for reading aloud with younger children, or for more experienced readers to enjoy independently, **Kingfisher Treasuries** offer a wonderful range of the very best writing for children. Carefully selected by an expert compiler, each collection reflects the real interests and enthusiasms of children. Stories by favourite classic and contemporary authors appear alongside traditional folk tales and fables in a lively mix of writing drawn from many cultures around the world.

Generously illustrated throughout, **Kingfisher Treasuries** guarantee hours of the highest quality entertainment and, by introducing them to new authors, encourage children to further develop their reading tastes.

KINGFISHER
An imprint of Kingfisher Publications Plc
New Penderel House, 283-288 High Holborn
London WC1V 7HZ

First published by Kingfisher 1992

5(5TR)/0898/SC/(MA)/USW 120

A CIP catalogue record for this book
is available from the British Library.

ISBN 0 86272 975 0

Printed in Hong Kong / China

A
TREASURY OF
Giant & Monster
Stories

CHOSEN BY JANE OLLIVER

ILLUSTRATED BY ANNABEL SPENCELEY

KING*f*ISHER

CONTENTS

THE SELFISH GIANT

Oscar Wilde

Every afternoon, as they were coming from school, the children used to go and play in the Giant's garden.

It was a large lovely garden, with soft green grass. Here and there over the grass stood beautiful flowers like stars, and there were twelve peach trees that in the springtime broke out into delicate blossoms of pink and pearl, and in the autumn bore rich fruit. The birds sat on the trees and sang so sweetly that the children used to stop their games in order to listen to them. "How happy we are here!" they cried to each other.

One day the Giant came back. He had been to visit his friend, the Cornish ogre, and had stayed with him for seven years. After the seven years were over, he had said all that he had to say, for his conversation was limited, and he determined to return to his own castle. When he arrived he saw the

children in the garden.

"What are you doing here?" he cried in a very gruff voice, and the children ran away.

"My own garden is my own garden," said the Giant. "Anyone can understand that, and I will allow nobody to play in it but myself." So he built a high wall around it, and put up a notice-board.

> TRESPASSERS
> WILL BE
> PROSECUTED

He was a very selfish Giant.

The poor children had now nowhere to play. They tried to play on the road, but the road was very dusty and full of hard stones, and they did not like it. They used to wander around the high walls when their lessons were over and talk about the beautiful garden inside. "How happy we were there!" they said to each other.

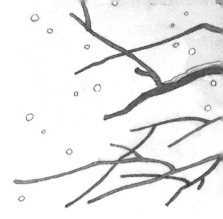

Then the spring came, and all over the country there were little blossoms and little birds. Only in the garden of the Selfish Giant it was still winter. The birds did not care to sing in it as there were no children, and the trees forgot to blossom. Once a beautiful flower put its head out from the grass, but when it saw the notice-board it was so sorry for the children that it slipped back into the ground again, and went off to sleep. The only people who were pleased were the Snow and the Frost. "Spring has forgotten this garden," they cried, "so we will live here all the year round." The Snow covered up the grass with her great white cloak, and the Frost painted all the trees silver. Then they invited the North Wind to stay with them, and he came. He was wrapped in furs, and roared all day about the garden, and blew the chimney pots down. "This is a delightful spot," he said. "We must ask the Hail on a visit." So the Hail came. Every day for three hours he rattled on the roof of the castle till he broke most of the slates, and then he ran around and around the garden as fast as he could go. He was dressed in gray, and his breath was like ice.

"I cannot understand why the spring is so late in coming," said the Selfish Giant, as he sat at the window and looked out at his cold, white garden. "I hope there will be a change in the weather."

But the spring never came, nor the summer. The fall gave golden fruit to every garden, but to the Giant's garden she gave none. "He is too selfish," she said. So it was always winter there, and the North Wind and the Hail, and the Frost, and the Snow danced about through the trees.

One morning the Giant was lying awake in bed when he heard some lovely music. It sounded so sweet to his ears that he thought it must be the King's musicians passing by. It was really only a little linnet singing outside his window, but it was so long since he had heard a bird sing in his garden that it seemed to him to be the most beautiful music in the world. Then the Hail stopped dancing over his head, and the North Wind ceased roaring, and a delicious perfume came to him through the open casement. "I believe the spring has come at last," said the Giant; and he jumped out of bed and looked out.

What did he see?

He saw the most wonderful sight. Through a little hole in the wall the children had crept in, and they were sitting in the branches of the trees. In every tree that he could see there was a little child. And the trees were so glad to have the children back again that they had covered themselves with blossoms, and were waving their arms gently above the children's heads. The birds were flying about and twittering with delight, and the flowers were looking up through the green grass and laughing. It was a lovely scene; only in one corner it was still winter. It was the farthest corner of the garden, and in it was standing a little boy. He was so small that he could not reach up to the branches of the tree, and he was wandering all around it, crying bitterly. The poor tree was still covered with frost and snow, and the North Wind was blowing and roaring above it. "Climb up, little boy!" said the Tree, and it bent its branches down as low as it could; but the boy was too tiny.

And the Giant's heart melted as he looked out. "How selfish I have been!" he said. "Now I know why the spring would not come here. I will put that poor little boy on the top of the tree, and then I will knock down the wall, and my garden shall be the children's playground for ever and ever." He was really very sorry for what he had done.

So he crept downstairs and opened the front door quite softly, and went out into the garden. But when the children saw him they were so frightened that they all ran away, and the garden became winter again. Only the little boy did not run, for his eyes were so full of tears that he did not see the Giant coming. And the Giant stole up behind him and took him gently in his hand, and put him up into the tree. And the tree broke at once into blossom, and the birds came and sang on it, and the little boy stretched out his two arms and flung them around the Giant's neck, and kissed him. And the other children, when they saw that the Giant was not wicked any longer, came running back, and with them came the Spring. "It is your garden now, little children," said the Giant, and he took a great ax and knocked down the wall. And when the people were going to market at twelve o'clock they found the Giant playing with the children in the most beautiful garden they had ever seen.

All day long they played, and in the evening they came to the Giant to bid him good-bye.

"But where is your little companion?" he said, "the boy I put into the tree." The Giant loved him the best because he had kissed him.

"We don't know," answered the children. "He has gone away."

"You must tell him to be sure and come tomorrow," said the Giant. But the children said that they did not know where he lived and had never seen him before, and the Giant felt very sad.

Every afternoon, when school was over, the children came and played with the Giant. But the little boy whom the Giant loved was never seen again. The Giant was very kind to all the children, yet he longed for his first little friend, and often spoke of him. "How I would like to see him!" he used to say.

Years went by, and the Giant grew very old and feeble. He could not play with the children anymore, so he sat in a huge armchair, and watched the children at their games, and admired his garden. "I have many beautiful flowers, he said, "but the children are the most beautiful flowers of them all."

One winter morning he looked out of his window as he was dressing. He did not hate the winter now, for he knew that it was merely the spring asleep, and that the flowers were resting.

Suddenly he rubbed his eyes in wonder and looked and looked. It certainly was a marvelous sight. In the farthest corner of the garden was a tree quite covered with lovely white blossoms. Its branches were golden, and silver fruit hung down from them, and underneath it stood the little boy he had loved.

Downstairs ran the Giant in great joy, and out into the

garden. He hastened across the grass, and came near the child. And when he came quite close his face grew red with anger, and he said, "Who hath dared to wound thee?" For on the palms of the child's hands were the prints of two nails, and the prints of two nails were on the little feet.

"Who hath dared to wound thee?" cried the Giant. "Tell me, that I may take my big sword and slay him."

"Nay," answered the child. "But these are the wounds of Love."

"Who art thou?" said the Giant, and a strange awe fell on him, and he knelt before the little child.

And the child smiled on the Giant, and said to him, "You let me play once in your garden; today you shall come with me to my garden, which is Paradise."

And when the children ran in that afternoon, they found the Giant lying dead under the tree, all covered with white blossoms.

THOR'S STOLEN HAMMER

A Viking Tale

"Where's my hammer?" roared Thor, the Viking God of Thunder. He had been looking everywhere for his precious hammer, Miolnir, since early morning. Miolnir had been made by a clever dwarf from a meteorite that had fallen from the sky during a great storm. With it and his iron gloves and magic belt, Thor was the most powerful of all the gods. It was he who made the thunder and lightning. It was he who broke up the winter ice so that spring could begin again. So Thor was furious when he found that his hammer had gone.

"Someone must have stolen it in the night," he shouted.

Loki, the mischievous god, heard him and said, "Miolnir must have been stolen by our enemies the giants. I'll go and find out for you." And at once he turned himself into a bird and flew off to the frozen lands of the giants.

Thrym, the King of the Giants, was sitting on a mound of ice, idly tossing snowballs at the trees. He was bored, and even Loki was better than no one at all to talk to.

"What brings you here, Loki?" he asked.

"I am searching for Thor's lost hammer," replied Loki. "Do you know where it is?"

Thrym burst out laughing.

"Of course I do! I took the Thunderer's hammer and I've hidden it deep underground where no one but me can find it."

"But it's of no use to you," said the cunning Loki. "What would you take in exchange for it?"

21

Thrym smiled, which was not a pretty sight as he had hideously bad teeth.

"Tell Thor that if I can have the beautiful goddess Freya for my wife, I will give the hammer to her as a wedding gift."

Loki flew back to Thor as fast as he could.

"Thrym has your hammer," he reported to Thor, "but he will only give it back if he can marry Freya."

Thor was so eager to recover his precious Miolnir that he rushed off to Freya, shouting, "Freya! Get ready to marry Thrym the Giant, right now."

Freya glared at him and said, "Don't be silly. I am married already. In any case, I would never agree to wed that revolting old giant. How dare you even suggest such a thing!"

Then Thor felt rather ashamed of himself and called all the other gods to a meeting in the palace of Odin, his father, to decide what could be done. The gods all talked for a long time until at last Loki said, "I have thought of a plan. Thrym wants Freya as his bride. If Thor shaves off his beard and disguises himself as a woman, he can go in her place. He can wear a bridal veil and a long white robe adorned with plenty of brooches and jewels."

"Dress as a woman!" roared Thor, banging the table with his fist so that sparks flew. "Never! I would die of shame."

"Nonsense, my son," said Odin firmly. "Loki can go with you as the bridesmaid. The giants will not

laugh at you when you have your hammer again and can kill them with it."

So, very reluctantly, Thor agreed to disguise himself as Freya, and with Loki dressed up as the bridesmaid, the pair of them set off in Thor's chariot.

Thrym the Giant was delighted when he saw two veiled figures approaching his castle. As he helped Freya from the chariot he was rather surprised to see how tall she was and what great muscles there were on her arms. But he was too excited to worry about it. Later, when the wedding banquet was served, Thrym was astonished to see his bride eat a whole ox, eight salmon and several platefuls of cakes. She drank three barrels of mead too.

"I've never seen such an appetite as yours, my dear," he exclaimed. "Do you always eat so much?"

Thor did not know what to say, but Loki answered for him in a high voice, "Freya has been fasting for eight days so that she could look her best for you."

"Bless her little heart!" exlaimed Thrym. "That deserves a kiss." And he leaned forward to raise his bride's veil. Thor was so horrified he sprang up, his eyes flashing.

"My dear, how your eyes flash and flame! What is wrong?" Thrym asked.

Again Loki piped up for Thor, saying, "Freya has not slept for eight days and nights because she was so excited about coming here."

Thrym was as pleased with this explanation as the last.

"Let's get on with the wedding!" he exclaimed. "Bring in my present for the bride."

The hammer Miolnir was carried in and placed upon the bride's lap. At once, Thor seized it and threw off his disguise. With one blow, he slew Thrym and then any other giant who dared to approach him. The rest fled in terror.

With Miolnir safe in their hands, Thor and Loki rode joyfully back, over the rainbow bridge, to the home of the gods.

Odin had been right. Not one of the giants had laughed at Thor. He had fooled them all.

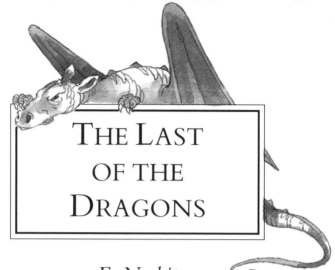

THE LAST
OF THE
DRAGONS

E. Nesbit

Of course you know that dragons were once as common as motor-omnibuses are now, and almost as dangerous. But as every well-brought-up prince was expected to kill a dragon, and rescue a princess, the dragons grew fewer and fewer, till it was often quite hard for a princess to find a dragon to be rescued from. And at last there were no more dragons in France and no more dragons in Germany, or Spain, or Italy, or Russia. There were some left in China, and are still, but they are cold and bronzy, and there were never any, of course, in America. But the last real dragon left was in England, and of course that was a very long time ago, before what you call English History began. This dragon lived in Cornwall in the big caves amid the rocks, and was a very fine big dragon, quite seventy feet long from the tip of its fearful snout to the end of its terrible tail. It breathed fire and smoke, and rattled when it walked, because its scales were made of iron. Its wings were like half-umbrellas – or like bat's wings, only several thousand times bigger. Everyone was very frightened of it, and well they might be.

Now the King of Cornwall had one daughter, and when she was sixteen, of course she would have to go and face the dragon: such tales are always told in royal nurseries at twilight, so the Princess knew what she had to expect. The dragon would not eat her, of course – because the prince would come and rescue her. But the Princess could not help thinking it would be much pleasanter to have nothing to do with the dragon at all – not even to be rescued from him.

"All the princes I know are such very silly little boys," she told her father. "Why must I be rescued by a prince?"

"It's always done, my dear," said the King, taking his crown off and putting it on the grass, for they were alone in the garden, and even kings must unbend sometimes.

"Father, darling," said the Princess presently, when she had made a daisy chain and put it on the King's head, where the crown ought to have been. "Father, darling, couldn't we tie up one of the silly little princes for the dragon to look at – and then *I* could go and kill the dragon and rescue the Prince? I fence much better than any of the princes we know."

"What an unladylike idea!" said the King, and put his crown on again, for he saw the Prime Minister coming with a basket of newlaid Bills for him to sign. "Dismiss the thought, my child. I rescued your mother from a dragon, and you don't want to set yourself up above her, I should hope?"

"But this is the *last* dragon. It is different from all other dragons."

"How?" asked the King.

"Because he *is* the last," said the Princess, and went off to her fencing lessons, with which she took great pains. She took great pains with all her lessons – for she could not give up the idea of fighting the dragon. She took such pains that she became the strongest and boldest and most skilful and most sensible princess in Europe. She had always been the prettiest and nicest.

And the days and years went on, till at last the day came which was the day before the Princess was to be rescued from the dragon. The prince who was to do this deed of valour was a pale prince, with large eyes and a head full of mathematics and philosophy, but he had unfortunately neglected his fencing lessons. He was to stay the night at the palace, and there was a banquet.

After supper the Princess sent her pet parrot to the Prince with a note. It said:

"Please, Prince, come onto the terrace. I want to talk to you without anybody else hearing – The Princess."

So, of course, he went – and he saw her gown of silver a long way off, shining among the shadows of the trees like water in starlight. And when he came quite close to her he said.

"Princess, at your service," and bent his cloth-of-gold-covered knee and put his hand on his cloth-of-gold-covered heart.

"Do you think," said the Princess earnestly, "that you will be able to kill the dragon?"

"I will kill the dragon," said the Prince firmly, "or perish in the attempt."

"It's no use your perishing," said the Princess.

"It's the least I can do," said the Prince.

"What I'm afraid of is that it'll be the most you can do," said the Princess.

"It's the only thing I can do," said he, "unless I kill the dragon."

"Why you should do anything for me is what I can't see," said she.

"But I want to," he said. "You must know that I love you better than anything in the world."

When he said that, he looked so kind that the Princess began to like him a little.

"Look here," she said, "no one else will go out tomorrow. You know they tie me to a rock, and leave me – and then everybody scurries home and puts up the shutters and keeps them shut till you ride through the town in triumph shouting that you've killed the dragon, and I ride on the horse behind you weeping for joy."

"I've heard that that is how it is done," said he.

"Well, do you love me well enough to come very quickly and set me free – and we'll fight the dragon together?"

"It wouldn't be safe for you."

"Much safer for both of us for me to be free, with a sword in my hand, than tied up and helpless. *Do* agree."

He could refuse her nothing. So he agreed. And next day everything happened as she had said.

When he had cut the cords that tied her to the rock, they stood on the lonely mountainside looking at each other.

"It seems to me," said the Prince," "that this ceremony could have been arranged without the dragon."

"Yes," said the Princess, "but since it has been arranged with the dragon – "

"It seems such a pity to kill the dragon – the last in the world," said the Prince.

"Well, then, don't let's," said the Princess. "Let's tame it not to eat princesses but to eat out of their hands. They say everything can be tamed by kindness."

"Taming by kindness means giving them things to eat," said the Prince. "Have you got anything to eat?"

She hadn't, but the Prince owned that he had a few biscuits. "Breakfast was so very early," said he, "and I thought you might have felt faint after the fight."

"How clever," said the Princess, and they took a biscuit in each hand. And they looked here and they looked there, but never a dragon could they see.

"But here's its trail," said the Prince, and pointed to where the rock was scarred and scratched so as to make a track leading to the mouth of a dark cave. It was like cart-ruts in a Sussex road, mixed with the marks of sea gulls' feet on the sea sand. "Look, that's where it's dragged its brass tail and planted its steel claws."

"Don't let's think how hard its tail and its claws are," said the Princess, "or I shall begin to be frightened – and I know you can't tame anything, even by kindness, if you're frightened of it. Come on. Now or never."

She caught the Prince's hand in hers and they ran along the path toward the dark mouth of the cave. But they did not run into it. It really was so very *dark*.

So they stood outside, and the Prince shouted: "What ho! Dragon there! What ho within!" And from the cave they heard an answering voice and great clattering and creaking. It sounded as though a rather large cotton mill were stretching itself and waking up out of its sleep.

The Prince and the Princess trembled, but they stood firm.

"Dragon – I say, Dragon!" said the Princess. "Do come out and talk to us. We've brought you a present."

"Oh, yes – I know your presents," growled the dragon in a huge, rumbling voice. "One of those precious princesses, I suppose? And I've got to come out and fight for her. Well, I tell you straight, I'm not going to do it. A fair fight I wouldn't say no to – a fair fight and no favor – but one of these put-up fights where you've got to lose – No. So I tell you. If I wanted a princess I'd come and take her, in my own time – but I don't. What do you suppose I'd do with her, if I'd got her?"

"Eat her, wouldn't you?" said the Princess in a voice that trembled a little.

"Eat a fiddle-stick end," said the dragon very rudely. "I wouldn't touch the horrid thing."

The Princess's voice grew firmer.

"Do you like biscuits?" she asked.

"No," growled the dragon.

"Not the nice little expensive ones with sugar on the top?"

"*No*," growled the dragon.

"Then what *do* you like?" asked the Prince.

"You go away and don't bother me," growled the dragon, and they could hear it turn over, and the clang and clatter of its turning echoed in the cave like the sound of the steam-hammers in the Arsenal at Woolwich.

The Prince and Princess looked at each other. What *were* they to do? Of course it was no use going home and telling the King that the dragon didn't want princesses – because His Majesty was very old-fashioned and would never have believed that a new-fashioned dragon could ever be at all different from an old-fashioned dragon. They could not go into the cave and kill the dragon. Indeed, unless he attacked the Princess it did not seem fair to kill him at all.

"He must like something," whispered the Princess, and she called out in a voice as sweet as honey and sugar-cane.

"Dragon – Dragon dear!"

"WHAT?" shouted the dragon. "Say that again!" and they could hear the dragon coming towards them through the darkness of the cave. The Princess shivered, and said in a very small voice:

"Dragon – Dragon dear!"

And then the dragon came out. The Prince drew his sword, and the Princess drew hers – the beautiful silver-handled one that the Prince had brought in his motor-car. But they did not attack; they moved slowly back as the dragon came out, all the vast scaly length of him, and lay along the rock – his great

35

wings half-spread and his silvery sheen gleaming like diamonds in the sun. At last they could retreat no further – the dark rock behind them stopped their way – and with their backs to the rock they stood swords in hand and waited.

The dragon drew nearer and nearer – and now they could see that he was not breathing

fire and smoke as they had expected – he came crawling slowly towards them wriggling a little as a puppy does when it wants to play and isn't quite sure whether you're cross with it.

And then they saw that great tears were coursing down its brazen cheek.

"Whatever's the matter?" said the Prince.

"Nobody," sobbed the dragon, "ever called me 'dear' before!"

"Don't cry, dragon dear," said the Princess. "We'll call you 'dear' as often as you like. We want to tame you."

"I *am* tame," said the dragon – "that's just it. That's what nobody but you has ever found out. I'm so tame that I'd eat out of your hands."

"Eat what, dragon dear?" said the Princess. "Not biscuits?"

The dragon slowly shook its heavy head.

"Not biscuits?" said the Princess tenderly. "What, then, dragon dear?"

"Your kindness quite undragons me," it said. "No one has ever asked any of us what we like to eat – always offering us princesses, and then rescuing them – and never once, 'What'll you take to drink the King's health in?' Cruel hard I call it," and it wept again.

"But what would you like to drink our health in?" said the Prince. "We're going to be married today, aren't we, Princess?"

She said that she supposed so.

"What'll I take to drink your health in?" asked the dragon. "Ah, you're something like a gentleman, you are, sir. I don't mind if I do, sir. I'll be proud to drink your and your good lady's health in a tiddy drop of" – its voice faltered – "to think of you asking me so friendly like," it said. "Yes, sir, just a tiddy drop of puppuppuppuppupetrol – tha – that's what does a dragon good, sir – "

"I've lots in the car," said the Prince, and was off down the mountain like a flash. He was a good judge of character, and he knew that with this dragon the Princess would be safe.

"If I might make so bold," said the dragon, "while the gentleman's away – p'raps just to pass the time you'd be so kind as to call me Dear again, and if you'd shake claws with a poor old dragon that's never been anybody's enemy but his own – well, the last of the dragons'll be the proudest dragon there's ever been since the first of them."

It held out an enormous paw, and the great steel hooks that were its claws closed over the Princess's hand as softly as the claws of the Himalayan bear will close over the bit of bun you hand it through the bars at the Zoo.

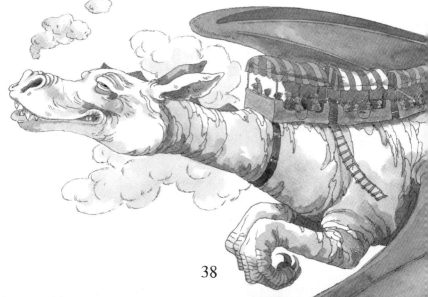

And so the Prince and Princess went back to the palace in triumph, the dragon following them like a pet dog. And all through the wedding festivities no one drank more earnestly to the happiness of the bride and bridegroom than the Princess's pet dragon – whom she had at once named Fido.

And when the happy pair were settled in their own kingdom, Fido came to them and begged to be allowed to make himself useful.

"There must be some little thing I can do," he said, rattling his wings and stretching his claws. "My wings and claws and so on ought to be turned to some account – to say nothing of my grateful heart."

So the Prince had a special saddle or howdah made for him – very long it was – like the tops of many tramcars fitted together. One hundred and fifty seats were fitted to this, and the dragon, whose greatest pleasure was now to give pleasure to others, delighted in taking parties of children to the seaside. It flew through the air quite easily with its hundred and fifty little passengers – and would lie on the sand patiently waiting till they were ready to return. The children were very fond of it and used to call it dear, a word which never failed to bring tears of affection and gratitude to its eyes. So it lived, useful and respected, till quite the other day – when someone happened to say, in his hearing, that dragons were out-of-date, now so much new machinery had come in. This so distressed him that he asked the King to change him into something less old-fashioned, and the kindly monarch at once changed him into a mechanical contrivance. The dragon, indeed, became the first aeroplane.

THE GIANT'S CLEVER WIFE

An Irish Tale

Finn McCoul was a giant who lived in the north of Ireland long ago. He was building a bridge across the sea to Scotland which, to this day, is called The Giant's Causeway. Now Finn wanted a sight of his wife Oonagh whom he loved dearly, so he pulled up a whole fir tree, lopped off its roots and branches to make a walking stick, and he set off. Clean over the mountain tops he stepped and was soon at home at the top of Knockmany Hill.

His wife greeted him with a great kiss. "It's pleased I am to see you. Sit down and have the fine dinner I've ready for you." Finn ate twenty eggs, a whole oxen, fifty cabbages, and a great pile of delicious loaves, hot from the oven.

They were happy together, chatting over this and that, but Oonagh saw that Finn was troubled. "Why are you putting that great thumb in your mouth?" says she. She knew that Finn was touching a special

41

tooth which could warn him of danger.

"It's himself is coming," says Finn. "It's Cucullin and doesn't he carry a thunderbolt with him that he flattened like a pancake with his fist?"

"Sure and you've beaten other giants, my fine husband," says Oonagh.

"Not one that shakes the entire country with one stamp of his foot. It's disgraced I'll be if I can't beat him," groaned Finn.

"Easy now. Go you and watch out over the mountains for this wee fellow," says Oonagh scornfully, "and by all the saints, I'll prepare a welcome for him. Indeed I will."

"You're a grand girl," declared Finn and out he went, leaving Oonagh to bake some very special loaves with iron griddles inside them. She was boiling a whole side of bacon when she heard a shout from Finn.

"He's coming and he's a terrible sight to see. It's a man-mountain he is. Glory be, I cannot fight him and him with that finger on him too." Everybody knew that all Cucullin's strength came from his forefinger and that without it he was just an ordinary man.

"Quiet, or you'll shame me," says Oonagh. "Now do as I tell you, my darling man, and put on this nightgown. And now this baby bonnet."

"Me! A baby. Never!" screeched Finn.

"Stop fussing, man, or it's flattened you'll be! Now into the children's old cradle with you."

Oonagh covered him with a quilt and pushed a baby's bottle into his mouth. "Lie there and trust me," Oonagh whispered. "He's coming."

She gave three long whistles, a sign that strangers are welcome, and sure enough, there came a knock on the door like thunder.

"Welcome stranger. Come along in," called Oonagh, "and sad it is that my husband isn't at home to greet you."

"Would that be the great Finn McCoul?" And Cucullin himself walked in. "I'm sorry he isn't here for I'm told he is the strongest man in Ireland and I'd love to have the sight of him."

"Not just now you wouldn't," Oonagh said. "Some bastoon of a giant called Cucullin has been threatening him and Finn has rushed off to the Giant's Causeway to teach this boyo a lesson."

"I'm Cucullin," this giant roared, "and I'll be teaching him a lesson, I'm thinking."

Oonagh laughed. "Did you ever see Finn? You'd better hope that his temper has cooled before you meet him, for he's much bigger and stronger than you. Sit you down and take a rest. You'll need all your strength if it's Finn you're after fighting."

She turned to the oven and pulled out the bread. "Ah now, if the wind isn't blowing right through the house. While you're waiting, would you just turn the house around for me," Oonagh asked. "That's one of the little things Finn does when he's at home."

Cucullin pulled on his forefinger then went outside, picked up the house and turned it away from the wind. Finn trembled in the cradle. What was his good wife thinking of, he wondered.

Oonagh didn't show her surprise at Cucullin's strength. "Thank you," she said. "Dinner is almost ready but not a drop of water can I give you. Finn was going to find a new spring right behind those rocks, but he left in such a terrible temper that he forgot about it. Could you do that little thing for me?"

Cucullin heard the water gurgling and knew his job was to crack open the mountain itself. He pulled his finger once, twice, nine times. Then he bent down and tore a huge hole right through the rocks. This hole is called Mumford's Glen even today.

Finn was terrified by Cucullin's strength but Oonagh calmly invited the giant to sit down and eat. She brought the side of bacon, fifty cabbages, a pile of her special flat loaves with iron griddles inside, and a barrel of butter.

Cucullin picked up a loaf and took a huge bite.

"Cinders and ashes," he thundered. "Here's two of my finest teeth gone. What's in this bread, woman?"

"Why, nothing," Oonagh said in surprise. "It's the very bread I make for Finn and doesn't he eat twelve loaves just for his tea! You'll not be beating Finn McCoul, I'm thinking."

Cucullin seized another loaf. "Thundering

thunderbolts, that's another two teeth gone." He was now in a terrible temper but Oonagh smiled sweetly. "It's glad I am that Finn's away for he'd kill you for sure."

The giant roared and stamped around the room. Finn let out a yell as Cucullin bumped into the cradle.

"Now see what you've done," Oonagh scolded. "If you can't eat a decent loaf of bread then at least keep quiet and don't go bothering Finn's little son."

She winked at Finn "Is it hungry you are, my pet?" and she gave him an extra special loaf without an iron griddle inside it.

"Flashes of fury," Cucullin growled, nursing his sore jaw as he watched Finn tear off chunks of bread and chew them with happy little noises.

"Is this truly Finn McCoul's son?"

"Indeed it is," Oonagh said proudly. "He only eats a few loaves each day but he is growing strong like his Daddy."

Cucullin was astonished. "That baby must have strong teeth if he can chew that terrible bread." This was Oonagh's chance! "Powerful strong, they are," she agreed. "You can feel them if you wish. You must put your forefinger right in, though, to feel the back ones. Open your mouth wide, little man." And Oonagh pushed Cucullin's finger right inside Finn's mouth.

Snip, snap. Finn bit off the finger. "You've tricked me," Cucullin bellowed as Finn jumped out of the cradle. He hit out with his enormous fists but all his strength had gone with that finger. He turned and ran, down Knockmany Hill and away over the mountains.

Finn watched him go; then he and his clever wife enjoyed a grand dinner in peace. After that, Finn went on building the Giant's Causeway across to Scotland; but maybe he should have asked Oonagh's advice for it never was finished even to this day.

JACK AND THE BEANSTALK

An English Tale

There was once a boy called Jack who was brave and quick-witted. He lived with his mother in a small cottage and their most valuable possession was their cow, Milky-White. But the day came when Milky-White gave them no milk and Jack's mother said she must be sold.

"Take her to market," she told Jack, "and mind you get a good price for her."

So Jack set out to market leading Milky-White by her halter. After a while he sat down to rest by the side of the road. An old man came by and Jack told him where he was going.

"Don't bother to go to the market," the old man said. "Sell your cow to me. I will pay you well. Look at these beans. Only plant them, and overnight you will find you have the finest bean plants in all the world. You'll be better off with these beans than with a cow or money. Now, how many is five, Jack?"

"Two in each hand and one in your mouth," replied Jack, as sharp as a needle.

"Right you are, here are five beans," said the old man and he handed the beans to Jack and took Milky-White's halter.

When he reached home, his mother said, "Back so soon, Jack? Did you get a good price for Milky-White?"

Jack told her how he had exchanged the cow for five beans and before he could finish his account, his mother started to shout and box his ears. "You lazy good-for-nothing boy!" she screamed, "How could you hand over our cow for five old beans? What will we live on now? We shall starve to death, you stupid boy."

She flung the beans through the open window and sent Jack to bed without his supper.

When Jack woke the next morning there was a strange green light in his room. All he could see from the window was green leaves. A huge beanstalk had shot up overnight. It grew higher than he could see. Quickly Jack got dressed and stepped out of the window right into the beanstalk and started to climb.

"The old man said the beans would grow overnight," he thought. "They must indeed be very special beans."

Higher and higher Jack climbed until at last he reached the top and found himself on a strange road.

Jack followed it until he came to a great castle where he could smell the most delicious breakfast. Jack was hungry. It had been a long climb and he had had nothing to eat since midday the day before. Just as he reached the door of the castle he nearly tripped over the feet of an enormous woman.

"Here, boy," she called. "What are you doing? Don't you know my husband likes to eat boys for breakfast? It's lucky I have already fried up some bacon and mushrooms for him today, or I'd pop you in the frying pan. He can eat you tomorrow, though."

"Oh, please don't let him eat me," pleaded Jack. "I only came to ask you for a bite to eat. It smells so delicious."

Now the giant's wife had a kind heart and did not really enjoy cooking boys for breakfast, so she gave Jack a bacon sandwich. He was still eating when the ground began to shake with heavy footsteps, and a loud voice boomed: "Fee, Fi, Fo, Fum."

"Quick, hide!" cried the giant's wife and she pushed Jack into the oven. "After breakfast, he'll fall asleep," she whispered. "That is when you must creep away." She left the oven door open a crack so that Jack could see into the room. Again the terrible rumbling voice came:

"Fee, Fi, Fo, Fum
I smell the blood of an Englishman,
Be he alive or be he dead,
I'll grind his bones to make my bread."

A huge giant came into the room. "Boys, boys, I smell boys," he shouted. "Wife, have I got a boy for breakfast today?"

"No, dear," she said soothingly. "You have got bacon and mushrooms. You must still be smelling the boy you ate last week."

The giant sniffed the air suspiciously but at last sat down. He wolfed his breakfast of bacon and

mushrooms, drank a great bucketful of steaming tea, and crunched up a massive slice of toast. Then he fetched a couple of bags of gold from a cupboard and started counting gold coins. Before long he dropped off to sleep.

Quietly Jack crept out of the oven. Carefully he picked up two gold coins and ran as fast as he could to the top of the beanstalk. He threw the gold down to his mother's garden and climbed after it. At the bottom he found his mother looking in amazement at the gold coins and the beanstalk. Jack told her of his adventures in the giant's castle and when she examined the gold she realized he must be speaking the truth.

Jack and his mother used the gold to buy food. But the day came when the money ran out, and Jack decided to climb the beanstalk again.

It was all the same as before, the long climb, the road to the castle, the smell of breakfast, and the giant's wife. But she was not so friendly this time.

"Aren't you the boy who was here before," she asked, "on the day that some gold was stolen from under my husband's nose?"

But Jack convinced her she was wrong and in time her heart softened again and she gave him some breakfast. Once more as Jack was eating, the ground shuddered and the great voice boomed "Fee, Fi, Fo, Fum." Quickly, Jack jumped into the oven.

As he entered, the giant bellowed:

"Fee, Fi, Fo, Fum
I smell the blood of an Englishman,
Be he alive or be he dead,
I'll grind his bones to make my bread."

The giant's wife put a plate of sizzling sausages before him, telling him he must be mistaken. After breakfast, the giant fetched a hen from a back room. Every time he said "Lay!" the hen laid an egg of solid gold.

"I must steal that hen, if I can," thought Jack, and he waited until the giant fell asleep. Then he slipped out of the oven, snatched up the hen and ran for the top of the beanstalk. Keeping the hen under one arm, he scrambled down as fast as he could.

Jack's mother was waiting but she was not pleased when she saw the hen.

"Another of your silly ideas, is it, bring an old hen when you might have brought us some gold? I don't know what is to be done with you?"

Then Jack set the hen down carefully, and commanded "Lay!" just as the giant had done. To his mother's surprise the hen laid an egg of solid gold.

Jack and his mother now lived in great luxury. But in time Jack became a little bored and decided to climb the beanstalk again.

This time he did not risk talking to the giant's wife in case she recognized him. He slipped into the kitchen when she was not looking, and hid himself in the log basket. He watched the giant's wife prepare breakfast and then he heard the giant's roar:

"Fee, Fi, Fo, Fum
I smell the blood of an Englishman,
Be he alive or be he dead,
I'll grind his bones to make my bread."

"If it's that cheeky boy who stole your gold and our magic hen, then I'll help you catch him," said the giant's wife. "Why don't we look in the oven? It's my guess he'll be hiding there."

You may be sure that Jack was glad he was not in the oven. The giant and his wife hunted high and low but never thought to look in the log basket. At last they gave up and the giant sat down to breakfast.

After he had eaten, the giant fetched a harp. When he commanded "Play!" the harp played the most beautiful music. Soon the giant fell asleep, and Jack crept out of the log basket. Quickly he snatched up the harp and ran. But the harp called out loudly, "Master, save me! Save me!" and the giant woke.

With a roar of rage he chased after Jack.

Jack raced down the road toward the beanstalk with the giant's footsteps thundering behind him. When he reached the top of the beanstalk he threw down the harp and started to slither down after it. The giant followed, and now the whole beanstalk shook and shuddered with his weight, and Jack feared for his life. At last he reached the ground, and seizing an axe he chopped at the beanstalk with all his might. *Snap!*

"Look out, mother!" he called as the giant came tumbling down, head first. He lay dead at their feet with the beanstalk on the ground beside them. The harp was broken, but the hen continued to lay golden eggs for Jack and his mother and they lived happily for a long, long time.

ASSIPATTLE AND THE GIANT SEA SERPENT

A Scottish Tale
retold by Virginia Haviland

Long ago in the north of Scotland there lived a well-to-do farmer. He and his good wife had seven sons and one daughter.

The youngest son was called Assipattle, because he liked to lie before the fire wallowing in the ashes. His older brothers laughed at him and treated him with cuffs and kicks. They made him sweep the floor, bring in peat for the fire, and do any other little job too low for them.

Assipattle would have been unhappy but for his sister, who loved him and was kind to him. She listened to his long stories about trolls and giants, and encouraged him to tell more. His brothers, on the other hand, threw clods at him, and ordered him to stop his lying tales. What angered them most was that Assipattle himself was always the great hero in his tales.

One day, something happened that made poor Assipattle very sad. A messenger came asking the farmer to send his pretty daughter to live in the King's house. She was to serve as maid to the beautiful Princess, who was the King's only child and much beloved.

Assipattle saw his sister go off, and he became silent and lonely.

After some time, another rider came by with the most terrible of tidings – that a giant sea serpent was drawing near the land. Hearing this, even the boldest hearts beat fast with fear.

True enough, a serpent came and turned his head toward the land. He opened his awful mouth and yawned horridly. And the noise of his jaws coming together again shook the earth and the sea. This he did to show that if he were not fed he would consume every living thing upon the land. He was well named the Master Sea Serpent – or the *Mester Stoorworm* – for he was the largest, the first, and the father of all the sea serpents.

Fear fell upon every heart, and there was weeping in the land. The King summoned his council and they sat together for three days. But they could find no way to turn the monster away.

At last, when the council was at its wits' end, the Queen appeared. She was a bold woman, and stepmother to the King's beloved daughter.

Sternly she spoke to the councillors: "You are all brave men and great warriors – when you have only men to face. But now you deal with a foe that laughs at your strength. You must take counsel with the sorcerer, who knows all things. It is not by sword and spear, but by the wisdom of sorcery that this monster can be overcome."

To this counsel the King and his men had to agree, although they disliked the sorcerer.

The sorcerer came in – a short and grisly man, looking like a goblin or bogle with his beard hanging down to his knees. He said that their question was a hard one, but he would give them counsel by sunrise.

Next day the sorcerer told the councillors that there was only one way to satisfy the sea serpent and to save the land. This was to feed the monster once a week with seven lovely lassies. "If this should not soon remove the monster," he said, "there will then be only one remedy – one so horrid that I must not mention it unless the first plan fails."

When people saw the serpent, they cried: "Is there no other way to save the land?"

Assipattle stared at the monster, and he was filled with rage and with pity. Suddenly he cried out: "Will no one fight the sea serpent and keep the lassies alive? I'm not afraid; I would fight the monster."

Everyone looked at Assipattle. "The poor bairn is mad," they said. His eldest brother gave him a kick and ordered him home to the ashes.

On their way home together, Assipattle persisted in saying that he would kill the monster. His brothers became so angry at what they thought was bragging that they pelted him with stones. Later, in the barn, they even tried to smother him with straw, but their father, coming by, saved him.

At supper, when their father objected to what the sons had done to their smaller brother, Assipattle answered: "You need not have come to my help. I could have fought them all. Aye, I could have beat every one of them had I wished."

They all laughed then and said: "Why did you not try?"

"Because I wanted to save my strength to fight the giant sea monster," said Assipattle.

Now over all the land there was weeping and wailing for the death of so many innocent lasses. If this went on, there would be no maidens left.

The council met again and called for the sorcerer. They demanded to know his second remedy.

The sorcerer raised his ugly head. "With cruel sorrow I say that the King's daughter herself must be given to the monster. Then only shall the monster leave our land."

The sorcerer pretended grief, but he knew it would please the Queen to be rid of the Princess.

A great silence filled the council chamber. At last the King arose – tall, grim, and sorrowful. He said: "She is my only child. She is my dearest on earth. She should be my heir. Yet, if her death can save the land, let her die."

The councillors had to agree – but they did so in sorrow, for the Princess was beloved by everyone. When the head of the council, with sore heart, was about to pronounce the new edict, the King's own guard, who had stood by him in many battles, now rose and said: "I ask that, if then the monster has not gone away, the sorcerer himself shall become the monster's next meal." The councillors gave such a shout of approval to this that the sorcerer paled and seemed to shrink.

The King asked for a delay of three weeks, so that he might make a proclamation. He would offer his

daughter to any champion who would drive away
the monster.

Messengers now rode to all the neighbouring
kingdoms, to announce that whosoever would, by
war or craft, remove the sea serpent from the land
should have the Princess
for his wife. With her
would be given also the
kingdom – to which she
was heir – and the King's
famous sword, Sicker-
snapper. That was the
sword with which the
great god Odin had
fought his foes and driven
them to the back side of
the world. No man had
any power against it.

Every young prince
and warrior was stirred
by the thought of a beautiful wife, a rich kingdom,
and so great a sword. But,
more than this, they were
horrified by the edict that
their beloved Princess was
to be given to the monster
unless someone drove it
away.

Assipattle, hearing all

this, sat among the ashes and said nothing.

Six-and-thirty champions rode to the King's palace, each one hoping to win the prize. But when they beheld the monster, lying out in the sea with his great mouth open, twelve of the number suddenly fell ill and were carried home. Twelve others were so terrified that they began to run away and never stopped till they reached their own lands. Only twelve stayed at the King's house, and these felt their hearts drop to their stomachs.

At the end of the three weeks, at evening before the great day when the Princess was to be sacrificed, the King gave a great supper. But it turned into a dreary feast; little was eaten, and less was said. There was no spirit of making fun, for everyone was thinking heavily of the morrow.

When all but the King and his faithful guard had gone to bed, the King opened the great seat on which he always sat. It was the high chair of state, and in it his most precious things were kept. He lifted out the great sword, Sickersnapper.

"Why take you out Sickersnapper?" asked the guard. "Your day for fighting is gone, my lord. Let Sickersnapper lie, my good lord. You are too old to wield her now."

"Wheest!" said the King in anger. "Or I'll try my sword on your body! Think you that I can see my only bairn devoured by a monster and not strike a blow for her? I tell you – and with my thumbs crossed on the edge of Sickersnapper I swear it – that I and this good sword both shall perish before my daughter die. And now, my trusty man, prepare my boat ready to sail, with her bow to sea. I will fight the serpent myself!"

At the farm that night the family made ready to set out on the morrow to see what would happen on the great day. All were to go but Assipattle, who must stay home to herd the geese.

As Assipattle lay in his corner that night, he found he could not sleep. His mind was filling with plans. And he heard his parents talking. His mother said: "I do not think I will go with you tomorrow. I am not able to go so far on my feet and I do not care to ride alone." His father replied, "You need not ride alone.

I'll take you behind me, on Swift-go. None will go so fast as we."

Next Assipattle heard his mother say to his father: "For the last five years I have begged you to tell me how it is that, with you, Swift-go outruns any other horse in the land, while if anyone else rides him he hobbles along like an old nag."

"Indeed, Good wife," said the good man, "I will not keep the secret from you longer. It is that when I want Swift-go to stand, I give him a clap on the left shoulder. When I want him to ride like any other horse, I give him two claps on the right. But when I want him to fly fast, I blow through the windpipe of

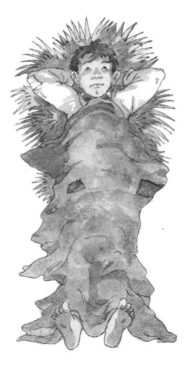

a goose. To be ready at any time, I always keep the pipe in the right-hand pocket of my coat. When Swift-go hears that, he goes swift as a storm of wind. So, now you know all. Keep your mind at peace."

Assipattle lay quiet as a mouse till he heard the old folk snoring. But then he did not rest long. He pulled the goose's windpipe out of his father's pocket, and slipped away fast to the stable. Swiftly he bridled Swift-go and led him out.

Knowing he was not held by his own master, Swift-go pranced and reared madly. But Assipattle remembered the secret and clapped his hand on Swift-go's left shoulder so that the horse stood still as a stone. Assipattle jumped on his back and clapped his right shoulder. And away they went.

As they were leaving, the horse gave a loud, loud neigh. This woke the farmer, who knew the cry of his horse. He saw Swift-go vanishing in the moonlight.

The farmer aroused his sons, and they all mounted and galloped after Swift-go, crying, "Thief!"

When Swift-go heard the farmer cry
"Hi, hi! ho!
Swift-go, whoa!"
he stopped for a moment. All would have been lost had not Assipattle pulled out the goose's windpipe. He blew through it with all his might. Swift-go heard this and went off like the wind, taking Assipattle swiftly beyond the others. The farmer and his sons had to return home.

As the day was dawning in the east, Assipattle saw

the sea and lying in it the giant sea serpent he had come to slay. He could see the monster's tongue jagged like a fork, with which it could sweep whatever it wanted into its mouth. But Assipattle had a hero's heart beneath his tattered rags – he was not afraid. I must be careful and do by my wits what I cannot manage by my strength, he thought.

Assipattle tethered his horse to a tree and walked till he came to a wee cottage. He found an old woman fast asleep in bed. He did not disturb her, but took down an old pot which he did not think she would mind his using to save the Princess's life. In the pot he placed a live peat from the fire.

Now, with pot and burning peat, he went to the shore. Near the water's edge he saw the King's boat with sails set and prow turned toward the monster. In the boat sat the man whose duty it was to watch till the King came.

"A nippy cold morning," said Assipattle to the man.

"Aye, it is that," said the man. "I have sat here all night till my very bones are frozen."

"Why don't you come on shore for a run, to warm yourself?" said Assipattle.

"Because," said the man, "if the King's guard found me out of the boat, he would half-kill me."

"Wise enough, " said Assipattle. "You like a cold skin better than a hot. But I must kindle a fire to roast a few mussels, for a hunger's like to eat a hole in my stomach."

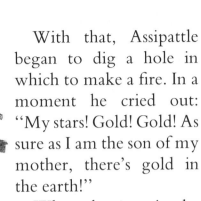

With that, Assipattle began to dig a hole in which to make a fire. In a moment he cried out: "My stars! Gold! Gold! As sure as I am the son of my mother, there's gold in the earth!"

When the man in the boat heard this, he jumped to shore and pushed Assipattle roughly aside. And while the man scraped about in the earth, Assipattle seized his pot, loosened the boat-rope, jumped into the boat, and pushed out to sea.

The outwitted man discovered what had happened and began to roar. And there was greater anger when the King arrived, carrying his great sword, Sickersnapper, in hopes of saving his daughter.

With the sun now peeping over the hills, the King and his company could only stand on shore and watch.

Assipattle had hoisted the sail and was steering for the head of the monster. The creature lay before him like an exceedingly big and high mountain, while the eyes of the monster glowed and flamed like a fire.

The sight might have terrified the bravest heart.

The monster's length stretched half across the world and his tongue was hundreds and hundreds of miles long. When in anger, he could with his tongue sweep whole towns, trees, and hills into the sea. His terrible tongue was forked, and he used the prongs as a pair of tongs with which to seize his prey. With that fork he could crush the largest ship like an eggshell. He could crack the walls of the biggest castle like a nut, and suck every living thing out of the castle into his mouth. Still, Assipattle had no fear.

74

Assipattle sailed up to the side of the serpent's head. Then, taking down his sail, he lay quietly on his oars, thinking his own thoughts. When the sun struck the monster's eyes, it gave a hideous yawn – the first of seven that it yawned before its awful breakfast. Each time the monster yawned, a great tide of sea water rushed down its throat and came out again through its huge gills.

Assipattle rowed close to the monster's head, with his sails down. At the second yawn, he and the boat were sucked in by the inrushing tide. But the boat did not stay in the monster's mouth. The tide carried her on, down a black throat that yawned like a bottomless pit. It was not very dark for Assipattle, for the roof and the sides of the tunnel were covered with a substance from the sea which gave a soft, silvery light in the creature's throat. On and on, down and down, went Assipattle. He steered his boat in midstream. As he went down, the water became more shallow, with part of it going out

through the gills. The top of the tunnel began to get lower, till the boat's mast stuck its end in the roof, and her keel stuck on the bottom of the throat.

Assipattle now jumped out. Pot in hand, he waded and ran, and began to explore, till he came to the monster's enormous liver. He cut a hole in the liver, and placed in it his live peat. He blew and blew on the burning peat till he thought his lips would crack. At length the peat began to flame. The flame caught the oil of the liver, and in a minute there was a large, hot fire.

Assipattle ran back to the boat as fast as his feet could carry him. When the serpent felt the heat of the fire, he began to cough. There arose terrible floods. One of these caught the boat and flung it, with Assipattle, right out – high and dry on the shore.

The King and all the people drew back to a high hill, where they were safe from the floods sent out by the monster. The serpent was indeed a terrible sight. After the floods of water, there came from its mouth and nose great clouds of smoke black as pitch. As the fire grew within the monster, it flung out its awful tongue and waved it to and fro until its end reached up and struck the moon. When the tongue fell back on the earth, it was so sudden and violent a fall that it cut the earth and made a long length of sea where there had been dry land. That is the sea that now divides Denmark from Sweden and Norway.

Now the serpent drew in his long tongue, and his

struggles and twisting were a terror to behold. The fiery pain made him fling up his head to the clouds. As his head fell back, the force of the fall knocked out a number of his teeth, and these teeth became the Orkney Islands. Again his head rose and fell, and he shed more of his teeth. These became the Shetland Islands. Finally the serpent coiled himself up into a great lump, and died. That lump became Iceland. And the fire that Assipattle kindled still burns in the mountains there.

And now everyone could plainly see that the monster was dead. The King took Assipattle in his arms and kissed him and blessed him and called him his son. He took off his own mantle and put it on Assipattle. And he girded on him the great sword, Sickersnapper. He took the Princess's hand and put it in Assipattle's hand, and he said that when the right time came the two should be married and Assipatle would rule over all the kingdom.

Assipattle mounted Swift-go and rode by the Princess's side. The whole company mounted their horses and returned with joy to the castle, where Assipattle's sister came running out to meet them.

Assipattle's sister told the King that the Queen and the sorcerer had fled on the two best horses in the stables. "They'll ride fast if I don't find them," said Assipattle. And with that, he went off like the wind on Swift-go, and soon caught up with the two. When the sorcerer saw Assipattle come so near, he said to the Queen: "It's only some boy. I'll cut off his head at once." But Assipattle drew Sicker-snapper, and with one dread thrust drove the sword through the sorcerer's heart. As for the Queen, she was brought back and made prisoner in a castle tower.

When Assipattle and the Princess were married there was a wedding feast that lasted nine weeks, as jolly as a feast in Yule. They became King and Queen and lived in joy and splendor. And, if not dead, they are yet alive.

THE GIANT WITH THREE GOLDEN HAIRS

Grimm Brothers

There was once a poor man whose only son was born under a lucky star – people said that the child would be blessed with good fortune and that he would grow up to be a wealthy man and would marry the sweetest, gentlest girl in the whole land.

Now the king of this land had a daughter who was not only beautiful but was also good and kind. Years passed, and the time came for the princess to be married. The king gave out a proclamation that said: "Any man who can descend into the wonderful cave and bring me three gold hairs from the head of the giant who lives there shall have my daughter's hand in marriage."

Princes and noblemen came from all over to try to win her hand, but they had little success.

Meanwhile the poor man's son had grown into a fine young man. One day, he happened to see the sweet princess as she passed by in her carriage and fell instantly in love with her. He decided to try for her hand and went at once to the king's palace.

The king was alarmed when he saw such a poor lad trying to win his daughter, but he said reluctantly: "Well, no one else has been successful, so you may as well try." Though he secretly hoped that the boy would fail.

So the young man set off on his journey to the wonderful cave. At the first city he came to, the guard of the gates into the city stopped him and asked: "Be so good as to tell us why our fountain in the marketplace is dry and will give no water, and we will reward you with gold." The young man promised he would on his return from the wonderful cave.

He came to a great kingdom and there the guard asked him: "Tell us why a tree which used to bear us golden apples, does not even produce a leaf and we will reward you with silver." The youth promised he would on his return.

The young man walked on until he came to a great lake which he knew he must cross. A ferryman agreed to take him and said: "Please tell me why I am bound forever to ferry people over this water and can never have any liberty, and I will reward you well." Again, the boy promised that he would on his return.

When he had crossed the lake he came at last to the wonderful cave, which looked dark and gloomy and full of foreboding. The brave lad was not to be deterred, however, and went boldly toward the cave. An old woman was sitting in a rocking chair at the entrance.

"What do you seek?" she said.

"Three golden hairs from the giant's head," came the quick reply.

"It will be difficult, but I can see you are a man blessed with a lucky star. I am the giant's grandmother and I will help you."

"I also need to know why the city fountain is dry, why the tree that bore golden apples is now without leaves, and why the ferryman cannot leave his position," the young man added hurriedly.

"These are puzzling questions, but listen to what the giant says when he returns to the cave." With that the old woman swiftly changed him into an ant and hid him in the folds of her dress.

Nightfall came and the giant returned home.

"I can smell man's flesh," he boomed. He searched around the cave in vain. Finally, he laid his head on his grandmother's lap and fell asleep. The old woman waited until he began to snore deeply, then she seized one of his golden hairs and pulled it out. Instantly, the giant woke up and cried out: "Good grief! What are you doing woman?"

"I'm sorry," the grandmother replied, "I had a strange dream: I dreamed that the fountain in the marketplace of a city had dried up and would give no water. What could cause this?"

"That's easy," snorted the giant, "under a stone in the fountain sits a toad; if he is killed, the water will flow again." With that the giant promptly fell asleep.

The grandmother pulled out another golden hair. "Ouch!" screeched the giant.

"Oh, I'm sorry dear, but I had another strange dream," said the crafty old lady. "This time I was in a great kingdom and there was a beautiful tree that used to bear golden apples that now could not even produce a leaf. What could cause this?"

"Must you keep bothering me? At the root of the tree a mouse is gnawing. If this mouse is killed, the tree will bear golden apples again. Now, let me sleep."

The grandmother waited until he was snoring loudly again, then quickly pulled out the third golden hair. At this the giant jumped up and bellowed at the old woman.

"Sorry, sorry!" she cried. "But I had such a strange dream – I saw a ferryman who was fated to go back and forth over a lake and could never be given his liberty. How can he escape?"

To this the giant replied crossly, "If he were to give the rudder to another passenger, he would be free, and the passenger would have to take his place." With this, the giant fell asleep.

The giant went out again early next morning. His grandmother turned the ant back into the young man and gave to him the three golden hairs and told

him to be on his way. The young lad joyfully
thanked the woman for all her help and ran quickly
away.

He soon came to the ferryman who agreed to take
him across the lake. As the young man got out of the
boat he said: "Give your rudder to any passenger
and then run away and you will be free." The
ferryman thanked him and the young man went on
his way.

He came next to the great kingdom with the
barren tree. He said to the guard: "Kill the mouse
that gnaws the root of the tree and the golden apples
will grow again." The guard thanked him and
rewarded him with silver.

The young man then came to the city with the
dried-up fountain. He said to the guard there: "Kill

the toad that sits under a stone in the fountain, and water will flow." The guard thanked him happily and the boy was rewarded with gold.

At last this child of fortune reached the king's palace and presented the three golden hairs on a velvet cushion to the king. The king was dismayed to see that the youth had fulfilled the task. "This is all very well," he said, "but I'm afraid you are not good enough for my daughter – you are too poor. You cannot marry her".

The young man cried out in anger at the king and then showed him all the gold and silver he had earned on his journey. "See, Sir, I am not as poor as you may think, and after all, you did give your word."

At the sight of all these riches the greedy king demanded to know where he had found them.

"On the side of a great lake, Sir," said the youth quickly. "If you ask the ferryman to take you across, you will see mountains of gold and silver on the other side."

The king didn't wait to hear any more, he rushed off to the great lake and got into the boat with the ferryman, who quickly gave him the rudder and sprang ashore, leaving the king to ferry back and forth for evermore.

Meanwhile, the sweet princess readily agreed to marry the young man and they lived in peace and happiness for the rest of their lives.

BEAUTY AND THE BEAST

Madame de Beaumont

Once upon a time a rich merchant lived with his six sons and six daughters in a big house in the city. The boys were handsome and clever and the girls were pretty and clever, but the youngest child was the happiest and the prettiest and everyone called her "Beauty". Her sisters did not like this and were very jealous. They loved going to parties, trying on new clothes, and visiting friends every day, and they laughed at Beauty who liked to stay at home reading or walking around her father's gardens.

Then suddenly the merchant's business failed and he lost all his money. He had to move with his children to a poky little house in a dark wood. No grand friends visited them now. There were no more parties and all the children had to work hard to earn money for food. Their clothes became tattered and they were often cold and hungry.

"It's all Father's fault," said the eldest sister.

"My hands are so rough," moaned the second.

"It's so dull here," declared the third.

"I hate the country," wailed the fourth.

"If only we had some new dresses," sighed the fifth.

"We could pick some flowers and make the cottage look pretty," said Beauty cheerfully, but her sisters went on grumbling.

After a while, the merchant heard that some of his money had been saved after all.

"I must go and see for myself," he declared.

"Take us with you," the children shouted, but he decided to go alone.

"Bring back dresses, perfume, jewellery, a carriage, and horses," the other sisters cried, but Beauty said nothing.

"And what would you like, Beauty?" her father asked.

"Simply your safe return," she answered quietly.

"Stupid girl," scolded her eldest sister, but her father held up his hand. "Thank you, daughter, but there must be something you'd like, isn't there?"

Beauty hesitated. "Well, I love roses and as none grow here, perhaps you could bring back just one rose for me?"

The merchant set off on his horse in high spirits, but when he arrived in the city there was only disappointment for he found that all his money had been stolen. He had to set off for home with nothing except his poor old horse. As he rode along, a terrible snowstorm broke overhead. The merchant was cold and wet when he came to the edge of the forest, but he decided to try and reach home before nightfall. His horse stumbled through the deepening snow and at last stopped, for all the paths were now covered up. The merchant was in despair for it was growing dark and he was lost. Suddenly he noticed some very faint marks between the trees. Leading his horse carefully, he struggled along until all at once he found himself in a wide avenue of trees, all covered with flowers and fruit. The snow had vanished and instead he saw an enormous castle with wide open doors just in front of him. He led his horse through the doors and into a stable, then entered the castle. How warm and comfortable it was! He peered into many rooms, all filled with magnificent furniture and treasure. The merchant was a little worried that

there was no one about, for he didn't want to seem rude or inquisitive. At last he came to a small room where a fire was blazing and delicious food was laid upon the table.

"I'll just dry my clothes and warm myself," he said to himself. "This food must be ready for someone, so I'll wait for the master or his servants to come. He waited and waited until it was quite dark outside. By now he was very hungry so he ate a little food. Then he saw a comfortable bed in the next door room and he fell asleep.

The next morning, when the sun woke him up, he found a new set of clothes on a chair and a tray with fruit and hot chocolate nearby. Nobody came in and the castle was silent.

"Thank you, whoever you are, for your kindness," the merchant called as he went to saddle his
horse. He passed some sweetly-scented rosebushes
and this made him remember his promise to Beauty.
He had just picked one lovely rose when there was a
terrible roar and a horrible Beast appeared. "I saved
your life," the Beast shouted in a fearsome voice,
"by giving you food and shelter. In return, you are
stealing my precious roses. You are an ungrateful
man, and for this you shall die."

The merchant threw himself on his knees. "I tried
to thank you, kind sir," he stammered. "I didn't

mean to upset anyone. I was going home empty-handed except for this rose." Then he poured out all his troubles to the Beast, and told him about his promise to Beauty. "Please spare me, at least until I've seen my family again."

The Beast glared at him, then said slowly, "I will forgive you on one condition. One of your daughters in exchange for you! She must come gladly and willingly and be brave enough to give her life for you. If none of your daughters is willing, then *you* must return within three months. Swear to keep this promise."

The merchant promised at once, certain that he'd return himself, for it was impossible to give a daughter to this monster.

"You must go know," the Beast ordered. "But first fill a chest in the castle hall with anything you like, and it will be delivered to you. Remember your promise." With these words, the Beast crashed away through the bushes. The merchant quickly found a big chest which he filled with gold and jewels. "At least my children will have money now," he sighed, "even though I must leave them forever."

His horse was waiting at the castle gate with one perfect rose fastened to the saddle. Before long, the merchant reached home. All the children rushed out to greet him. Their father hugged them, but he looked sad as he handed the rose to Beauty.

"This is a most unhappy gift," he sighed, and told them of his adventures and his promise to the Beast.

"Stupid Beauty," screamed the other sisters. "Why didn't you ask for gold? Now Father must die for you and we will have nothing."

Beauty took her father's hand. "I will gladly offer myself to this Beast to prove my love for you."

"No, little sister," cried her brothers. "We will find this creature and kill him. Then you'll both be safe."

The merchant shook his head. "He is too powerful for you. Besides, I made a promise."

"Which I will keep," said Beauty quietly.

When the merchant went upstairs to rest, he found the chest full of treasure by his bed. "The Beast kept his word," he thought. "If he is so generous, perhaps he will spare Beauty's life."

Her brothers begged Beauty to change her mind, but she would not, so after three months she got ready for the journey through the forest. Her brothers were very sad, but her sisters were very happy with the gold from the chest and only pretended to be upset.

Beauty and her father set off on their old horse and soon reached the castle. The merchant led Beauty across the hall, which was blazing with lights, into a small room where a splendid feast awaited them. She was hungry after the ride, but her father was too miserable to eat. Suddenly there was a great crash, and the Beast stood before them. Beauty shook with fear at the sight of him, but she curtsied bravely, "Gggg ... good evening, Beast."

The Beast was surprised.

"Were you forced to come here? Will you stay here without your father?"

"Yes, I will keep my promise," Beauty replied shakily.

"That pleases me," said the Beast, and then he turned to Beauty's father. "You must leave at dawn tomorrow. But first fill the boxes behind you and they will be sent to you."

He vanished. Beauty held her father's hand tightly before helping him to fill box after box with gold and jewels. Then, tired out, they both fell asleep. In her dreams a fairy came to Beauty.

"You have a kind heart," she said. "Don't be sad when your father goes. And, most of all, do not think only of the outside of things."

Next morning, after breakfast, the merchant sadly begged Beauty to let him stay in her place. But Beauty kissed him and almost pushed him onto his horse. Then she turned away and quickly ran into the castle to hide her tears.

Inside, each room seemed more beautiful than the last. In one she found a picture of a handsome prince with a kind smile, and in another there was a locket with the same picture inside, which Beauty hung around her neck. She saw no one all day, yet in the evening a delicious supper was ready for her beside a glowing fire in the little room.

As Beauty was eating, the Beast appeared. Was he going to kill her now? She held her breath, but he only said gruffly, "Good evening. What have you been doing since your father left?" At once Beauty told him about all the wonderful things she'd seen, and, as she talked, she forgot to be frightened.

"Will you be happy here?" the Beast asked after a while. "You can do whatever pleases you, at any time." There was a pause, then he added, "Do you think I'm very ugly?"

Beauty was terrified. What should she say? At last she replied gently, "I'm afraid I do."

The Beast sighed like the wind roaring.

"Well, enjoy your supper and I'll see you tomorrow," and he lumbered away.

That night the fairy visited Beauty again in her sleep. This time she was standing near the Prince's portrait. "Do not trust your eyes alone," she

whispered before vanishing.

The next day Beauty explored the gardens; they were filled with flowers, fountains, and singing birds, but there was not a gardener to be seen. At suppertime the Beast appeared again with a great roar and asked if she had enjoyed herself. Beauty chatted about the gardens and forgot to be frightened, until suddenly the Beast asked in his terrible voice, "Beauty, do you love me? Will you marry me?"

"Oh, Beast." She was very upset. "I'm afraid I don't love you." The Beast groaned like the roaring of the wind and turned away, head down and very miserable.

Each night Beauty dreamed the same dream, and each day she looked at the Prince's picture before reading, playing the piano, picking flowers, or trying on the wonderful dresses she found in the cupboards. "I'm just like my sisters," she laughed to herself.

Beauty now enjoyed talking to the Beast, but each night he would ask the same question, "Will you marry me?" and each night Beauty would answer, "I wish I could. I'm your friend but I do not love you." She was truly sad every time the Beast turned away with a deep sigh.

Beauty was not unhappy, but day after day the castle seemed so empty that she grew very lonely and longed to see her family once more. She knew now that the Beast was kind and gentle, even though he looked so fierce, so that night she begged him to grant her wish.

"I promise to come back, dear Beast."

"I can refuse you nothing," replied the Beast, "even if it kills me."

"I kept my promise before. I only want to see my father again. I would never hurt you or try to kill you." And Beauty began to weep.

"Then go," said the Beast, "and fill those boxes over there with anything you want. They will be sent to you." Then he held out a ring. "Take this ring and after two months, turn it round on your finger and say you are ready to come back. Remember, if you break your promise, I will die."

Beauty filled the boxes with presents, but in her dreams that night the Prince looked ill and weary, and the fairy shook her head sadly and said nothing. It was so strange that Beauty woke suddenly. The Beast's ring was on her finger but she heard her father's voice and she knew she was at home. She rushed downstairs, kissed him and gave out all the lovely presents she'd packed.

While she was at home, Beauty did not once dream about the Prince. When the two months were up, her father begged her to stay. That night she dreamed she was in the castle gardens. She heard pitiful groans and saw the Beast lying under a tree, close to death. "The Beast will die tomorrow if you listen to your father," she heard the fairy whisper, and Beauty woke up, sad and frightened.

"I must go back," she told her family and she turned the ring, closed her eyes and said, "I wish to see the Beast again."

At once she was back in the castle, but it was all cold and dark. The flowers were drooping and the birds were silent. She ran along a path like the one in her dream and heard a feeble groan. There was the Beast lying deathly still.

"Oh, Beast, I've come back," Beauty cried, but the Beast did not move. She wept bitterly as she stroked his ugly head. "Please don't die, dear Beast. I can't bear to lose you. Your looks don't matter at all because I love you."

Instantly there was sweet music everywhere. She looked at the castle which was now bright with lights, then turned back to see the Prince of her dreams kneeling before her.

"Where is my poor Beast?" Beauty asked.

"Here, kneeling at your feet." The Prince smiled and took her hand. "A wicked fairy cast a spell on me and said I must stay like this – a monster – until a

beautiful girl agreed to marry me because she loved me for myself. Beauty, you have broken that spell.''

Now the fairy of Beauty's dream appeared. She clapped her hands and the Prince and Beauty found themselves back in the castle. In the hall, all their relatives and friends waited, gathered together by the fairy's magic. The Prince and Beauty were married that day. They forgave Beauty's unkind sisters and everybody lived happily together for very many years.

THE SPRIGHTLY TAILOR

A Celtic Tale

A sprightly tailor was employed by the great Macdonald, in his castle at Saddell, in order to make the laird a pair of trews, used in olden time. And trews being the vest and breeches united in one piece, and ornamented with fringes, were very comfortable, and suitable to be worn in walking or dancing. And Macdonald he said to the tailor that if he would make the trews by night in the church, he would get a handsome reward. For it was thought that the old ruined church was haunted, and that fearsome things were to be seen there at night.

The tailor was well aware of this, but he was a sprightly man, and when the laird dared him to make the trews by night in the church, the tailor was not to be daunted, but took it in hand to gain the prize. So, when night came, away he went up the glen, about half a mile distance from the castle, till he came to the old church. Then he chose him a nice

gravestone for a seat, and he lighted his candle and put on his thimble and set to work at the trews, plying his needle nimbly and thinking about the hire that the laird would have to give him.

For some time he got on pretty well, until he felt the floor all of a tremble under his feet, and looking about him, but keeping his fingers at work, he saw the appearance of a great human head rising up through the stone pavement of the church. And when the head had risen above the surface, there came from it a great, great voice. And the voice said: "Do you see this great head of mine?"

"I see that, but I'll sew this!" replied the sprightly tailor, and he stitched away at the trews.

Then the head rose higher up through the pavement, until its neck appeared. And when its neck was shown, the thundering voice came again and said: "Do you see this great neck of mine?"

"I see that, but I'll sew this!" said the sprightly tailor, and he stitched away at his trews.

Then the head and neck rose higher still, until the great shoulders and chest were shown above the ground. And again the mighty voice thundered: "Do you see this great chest of mine?"

And again the sprightly tailor replied: "I see that, but I'll sew this!" and stitched away at his trews.

And still it kept rising through the pavement until it shook a great pair of arms in the tailor's face and said: "Do you see these great arms of mine?"

"I see those, but I'll sew this!" answered the tailor, and he stitched hard at his trews, for he knew that he had no time to lose.

The sprightly tailor was taking the long stitches when he saw it gradually rising and rising through the floor until it lifted out a great leg and, stamping with it upon the pavement, said in a roaring voice: "Do you see this great leg of mine?"

"Aye, aye: I see that, but I'll sew this!" cried the tailor, and his fingers flew with the needle, and he took such long stitches that he was just come to the end of the trews when it was taking up its other leg. But before it could pull it out of the pavement, the sprightly tailor had finished his task, and, blowing out his candle and springing from off his gravestone, he buckled up and ran out of the church with the trews under his arm. Then the fearsome thing gave a load roar and stamped with both feet upon the pavement, and out of the church he went after the sprightly tailor.

Down the glen they ran, faster than the stream when the flood rides it, but the tailor had got the start and a nimble pair of legs, and he did not choose to lose the laird's reward. And though the thing roared to him to stop, yet the sprightly tailor was not the man to be beholden to a monster. So he held his trews tight and let no darkness grow under his feet, until he had reached Saddell Castle. He had no sooner got inside the gate and shut it than the apparition came up to it, and, enraged at losing his prize, struck the wall above the gate and left there the mark of his five great fingers. Ye may see them plainly to this day, if ye'll only peer close enough.

But the sprightly tailor gained his reward, for Macdonald paid him handsomely for the trews and never discovered that a few of the stitches were somewhat long.

THE LITTLE BULL CALF

A Folk Tale

Long, long ago, there was a boy whose father gave him a little bull calf. Now, because the boy's family was very poor, the little bull calf was more precious to the boy than gold. He loved the little bull calf and fed him with pieces of his own barley bread every day.

One day, the boy's father died. His mother married again, but the man was a cruel stepfather. He hated the boy and threatened to kill both him and the little bull calf. So the boy decided he must leave home, taking his bull calf with him.

They set off early next day and walked for a long, long time, until they were both tired and hungry. When they came to a house, the boy begged a crust of bread. He broke the bread in half and shared it with the little bull calf. At the next house he came to, he was given a little curd cheese. He was going to share this too, but the little bull calf said, "No, you must keep it for later. Soon we shall be going through a dark forest where there are wild beasts and a fiery dragon. I will kill the wild beasts, but the dragon will kill me."

"No, no!" cried the boy, flinging his arms around the little bull calf's neck. "He can't kill you."

"Yes, it must be so," insisted the calf. "But you must not be sad. This is what you must do. As soon as we reach the forest, climb up into the tallest tree you can find. You will be safe there from all the wild animals, except the monkeys. If they come after you, the curd cheese will save you. When the dragon has killed me, he will go back to his lair to rest; while he is gone, you must cut out one of my ribs. With this, you will be able to kill the dragon. Hit him with it and he will fall down dead. Then you must remember to cut out his tongue."

The boy did everything the little bull calf had told him. He climbed the tallest tree he could find and when the monkeys chased after him, he held up the curd cheese in his fist and said, "If you come any nearer, I will squeeze your heart as easily as I squeeze this stone."

The monkeys, seeing juice dripping from what they thought was a stone, all turned tail and ran away.

Meanwhile, the little bull calf was fighting all kinds of savage beasts in the forest. He won every battle against them, but when the fiery dragon came, the little bull calf was killed.

The boy waited for the dragon to go. Then he slid down the tree, cut out one of the little bull calf's ribs and went after the dragon. He had not gone far when he found a beautiful princess tied to a tree by her hair. No sooner had the boy set her free than he heard the dragon come roaring toward them.

The boy waited until he could feel the dragon's fiery breath on his face. Then, with a mighty blow, he hit the dragon with the little bull calf's rib and the dragon fell down dead. As it fell, the dragon opened its great jaws and bit off the little finger on the boy's right hand. But the boy still remembered to cut out the dragon's tongue. Bidding the princess farewell, the boy then set off to seek his fortune. But before he left the princess gave him her diamond ring as a parting gift.

It was not long before the old king came to the

forest. He was weeping bitterly, for he was sure that his daughter had been eaten by the dragon. Imagine his surprise and joy to find her alive and unharmed!

On their way back to the palace, the princess told her father how she had been saved by the boy.

"We must find this young man so that he can be rewarded," declared the king.

Messengers were sent throughout the land to find the young man who had a little finger missing, the

princess's diamond ring, and a dragon's tongue. Whoever could show the king all these three things would marry the princess and one day become king.

Hundreds of men, young and old, flocked to the palace. Many had a finger missing, some on their right hand, some on their left. Many also had rings, some set with diamonds and others set only with pieces of coloured glass. Many even brought the tongue of a wild animal. But not one of them

brought a dragon's tongue, so they were all turned
away.

At last the boy himself came, looking so worn and
ragged that the king thought he was a beggar and
ordered him to be sent away. Luckily, the princess
was standing at her window and saw the boy
leaving. She ran to the king, crying, "Father! He is
the boy who saved me and killed the dragon!"

The king could hardly believe his ears. Surely this
beggar was not the one! But he said, "Let him return
and show me the missing finger on his right hand,
your diamond ring, and the tongue of the fiery
dragon."

The boy was brought back to the palace at once and he showed the king all three things.

And so the boy married the beautiful princess and there was much rejoicing throughout the land. When the old king died, the boy became king in his place and ruled his country wisely. But he never forgot his beloved little bull calf, to whom he owed all his good fortune.

FRIGHTENING THE MONSTER IN WIZARD'S HOLE

Margaret Mahy

One day a truck load of bricks went over a bump and two bricks fell off into the middle of the road. They lay there like two newly laid oblong eggs, dropped by some unusual bird. A boy called Tom-Tom coming down the road stopped to look at them. He picked one up. It was a beautiful glowing orange-coloured brick and it seemed as if it should be used for something special, but what can you do that's special with only one brick or even two?

"Hey Tom-Tom!" called his friend Sam Bucket coming up behind him. "What are you doing with that brick?"

"Just holding it," Tom-Tom said, "holding it and thinking ..."

"Thinking what?"

"... thinking that I'd take it and throw it really hard at ..."

"At whom, Tom-Tom?"

"At the monster in Wizard's Hole."

Sam's eyes and mouth opened like early morning windows. "You'd be too scared."

"No, I wouldn't. That's what I'm going to do now."

Tom-Tom set off down the road with his bright orange brick. Sam Bucket did not see why Tom-

Tom should have all the glory and adventure. He grabbed the brick that was left in the middle of the road.

"Hang on Tom-Tom! I'm coming too."

"Okay!" said Tom-Tom grandly. "But don't forget it's my idea, so I'm going to throw first."

"Where're you two off to?" asked a farmer leaning over his gate.

"We're going to throw these bricks at the monster in Wizard's Hole," explained Tom-Tom.

"He's going to throw first and I'm going to throw next," cried Sam boastfully.

"You'd never dare!" cried the farmer.

"We're on our way now," they said together, strutting like bantam roosters along the sunny, dusty road.

120

"But how are you going to get the monster out of Wizard's Hole?" asked the farmer. "He hasn't looked out for years."

"I shall shout at him," declared Tom-Tom grandly. "I shall say, 'Come on, Monster, out you come!' and he'll have to come, my voice will be so commanding."

"I shall shout too," said Sam Bucket quickly. "'Come out, Monster,' I shall say. 'Come out and have bricks thrown at you.' My voice will be like a lion's roar. He'll have to come."

"Hang on a moment," said the farmer. "I've got a brick down here for holding my gate open. I'm coming too."

Off went Tom-Tom, Sam Bucket, and the farmer, all holding bricks, all marching with a sense of purpose. They passed Mrs Puddenytame's pumpkin farm. Mrs Puddenytame herself was out subduing the wild twining pumpkins.

"You lot look pleased with yourselves," she remarked as they went by.

"We are," said Tom-Tom, "because we're on our way to do great things. You see these bricks? We're on our way to throw them at the monster in Wizard's Hole."

"You'd never dare!" breathed Mrs Puddenytame. "Why, they say that the monster is all lumpy and bumpy, horrible, hairy, and hideous – and besides, he hasn't bothered anyone for a hundred years."

"He's there, isn't he?" asked Sam Bucket. "'Come out,' we'll say. 'Out you come, Monster, and have bricks thrown at you.'"

"He'll have to come," cried the farmer. "And when he feels our bricks he'll run like a rabbit. We'll be heroes to the whole country."

"Well, hang on then!" Mrs Puddenytame shouted. "I've got a few spare bricks myself – and seven sons too." And she hunted the sons out of the pumpkins shouting, "Come on you louts! You can be heroes too."

"But mother," said her eldest, cleverest son,

"nobody else wants Wizard's Hole. Why shouldn't the monster stay there?"

"He's a monster isn't he?" yelled Mrs Puddeny-tame. "Whoever heard of rights for monsters? You get a brick and come along with the rest of us." Off they went, eleven people all carrying bricks down the sunny dusty road to town.

Once they got to town people came out of their houses to watch them. People followed them down the road. There was quite a procession by the time they reached the town square with the fountain in the middle of it. There Tom-Tom made a speech.

"Friends," he cried, "the time has come to act. We are going to throw bricks at the monster in Wizard's Hole."

"We're going to roar like lions," added Sam Bucket.

"And stamp like bulls!" agreed the farmer, stamping.

"We're going to laugh like hyenas, and shriek like mad parrots," Mrs Puddenytame shouted, "and frighten the monster into the next country. We've had the monster for too long. Let someone else have him."

"Hooray!" shouted all the people.

"The monster will run . . ." promised Tom-Tom.

"He'll flee!" agreed Sam Bucket.

"He'll fly!" gloated the farmer.

"He'll bound and pound and turn head over head over heels!" declared Mrs Puddenytame weighing her brick in her hand.

"I think I'll get a brick too," said the mayor thoughtfully, looking at a truckload of bricks parked by a building construction site. "Nothing should be done without a mayor."

"Don't forget the school children!" cried an anxious teacher. "Remember they're the citizens of tomorrow."

"But what are we doing it for?" asked a small child surprised.

"For the good of the community. Go and find a brick," commanded the teacher.

Soon everyone had taken a brick from the back of the truck and was marching sternly toward Wizard's hole.

The monster was just sitting down to a breakfast of fried eggs and crisp bacon when he heard the sound of many feet marching toward his front door.

"Visitors – at last!" thought the monster. He rushed to his bed cave, put on a collar and tie, washed behind his ears and brushed his many teeth. Then he ran to his front door and put his head out of Wizard's Hole.

"Good morning!" he said and smiled. Everyone

stopped. Tom-Tom stopped, Sam Bucket stopped. The farmer, Mrs. Puddenytame and her seven sons, the mayor, and the school teacher – everyone stopped.

"Come on in ... I'm just making fresh coffee." The monster smiled again showing his newly brushed teeth. He had a lot of teeth, this monster, many of them green and all of them sharp. Everyone stared.

"Do come in. I'm so pleased to see you," wheedled the monster. But the monster was wheedling in monster language, which is a mixture of growling, whining, roaring, and shrieking. Every single person dropped his brick. Every single solitary person ran without looking back once.

"Goodness me!" said the monster looking at the bricks. "Are all these presents for me? Too kind! Too kind! Thank

126

you . . ." he called after them. But he said the Thank-you in monster language, which is a mixture of rumbling, snarling, and screaming. Everyone ran even faster than ever before.

The monster went in and put on his bricklayer's apron, got his bricklayer's trowel and made himself a handsome brick monster house. Then he moved out of Wizard's Hole, which had always been so damp that the wallpaper peeled off, and he lived happily ever after.

And when Tom-Tom heard what had happened he said: "Well, we got him out of Wizard's Hole anyway."

And felt very successful.

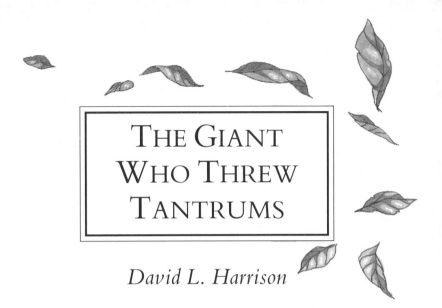

THE GIANT
WHO THREW
TANTRUMS

David L. Harrison

At the foot of Thistle Mountain lay a village.
In the village lived a little boy who liked to go
walking. One Saturday afternoon he was walking in
the woods when he was startled by a terrible noise.

He scrambled quickly behind a bush.

Before long a huge giant came stamping down
the path.

He looked upset.

"Tanglebangled ringlepox!" the giant bellowed.
He banged his head against a tree until the leaves
shook off like snowflakes.

"Franglewhangled whippersnack!" the giant
roared. Yanking up the tree, he whirled it around his
head and knocked down twenty-seven other trees.

Muttering to himself, he stalked up the path
toward the top of Thistle Mountain.

The little boy hurried home.

"I just saw a giant throwing a tantrum!" he told

everyone in the village.

They only smiled.

"There's no such thing as a giant," the mayor assured him.

"He knocked down twenty-seven trees," said the little boy.

"Must have been a tornado, or something. Happens around here all the time."

The next Saturday afternoon the little boy again went walking. Before long he heard a terrible noise. Quick as lightning, he slipped behind a tree.

Soon the same giant came storming down the path. He still looked upset.

Suddenly he threw himself on his face and pounded the ground with both fists.

Boulders bounced like hailstones.

Scowling, the giant puckered his lips into an "O."

He drew in his breath sharply. It sounded like somebody slurping soup.

"Pooh!" he cried.

Grabbing his left foot with both hands, the giant hopped on his right foot up the path toward the top of Thistle Mountain.

The little boy hurried home.

"That giant's at it again," he told everyone. "He threw such a tantrum that the ground trembled."

"Must have been an earthquake," the police chief said. "Happens around here sometimes."

The next Saturday afternoon the boy again went walking. Before long he heard a frightening noise.

He dropped down behind a rock.

Soon the giant came fuming down the path. When he reached the little boy's rock, he puckered his lips into an "O." He drew in his breath sharply with a loud, rushing-wind sound. "Phooey!" he cried. "I *never* get it right!"

The giant held his breath until his face turned blue and his eyes rolled up. "Fozzlehumper backawacket!" he panted. Then he lumbered up the path toward the top of Thistle Mountain.

The little boy followed him. Up and up and up he climbed to the very top of Thistle Mountain.

There he discovered a huge cave. A surprising sound was coming from it. The giant was crying!

"All I want is to whistle," he sighed through his tears. "But every time I try, it comes out wrong!"

The little boy had just learned to whistle. He knew how hard it could be. He stepped inside the cave.

The giant looked surprised. "How did *you* get here?"

"I know what you're doing wrong," the little boy said.

When the giant heard that, he leaned down and put his hands on his knees.

"Tell me at once!" he begged.

"You have to stop throwing tantrums," the little boy told him.

"I promise!" said the giant, who didn't want anyone to think he had poor manners.

"Pucker your lips . . ." the little boy said.

133

"I always do!" the giant assured him.

"Then blow," the little boy added.

"Blow?"

"Blow."

The giant looked as if he didn't believe it. He puckered his lips into an "O." He blew. Out came a long, low whistle. It sounded like a railway engine. The giant smiled.

He shouted, "I whistled! Did you hear that? I whistled!"

Taking the little boy's hand he danced in a circle.

"You're a good friend," the giant said.

"Thank you," said the little boy. "Perhaps some time we can whistle together. But just now I have to go. It's my suppertime."

The giant stood before his cave and waved good-bye.

The little boy seldom saw the giant after that. But the giant kept his promise about not throwing tantrums.

"We never have earthquakes," the mayor liked to say.

"Haven't had a tornado in ages," the weatherman would add.

Now and then they heard a long, low whistle somewhere in the distance.

"Must be a train," the police chief would say.

But the little boy knew his friend the giant was walking up the path toward the top of Thistle Mountain – whistling.

KING CALAMY AND THE DRAGON'S EGG

John Cunliffe

It was in the time of King Calamy the First that the Royal Dragon grew too old to fight.

"The poor old thing's so old that he cannot even run, never mind flying or spurting fire," said King Calamy to his Queen. "His days of glory are over. If we had to do battle with anyone he'd surely be killed, and what a disgrace that would be. Whatever shall we do?"

"Quite simple, my love," said the Queen. "Get a new dragon, and put the old one out to grass."

"Get a new dragon? A *new* one? And where in the kingdom do you suggest I should find a new dragon, my sweet?" demanded the king. "You seem to forget that we have had old Krog for nine hundred and ninety-nine years! Things were very different in the old days, when King Rongob caught Krog as a baby dragon, and brought him here to be tamed and taught to fight our enemies. There were

136

more dragons about then – the history books are full of them. They're a dying race, my dear; a thing of the past!"

"Nonsense," said the Queen. "Only last week, young Lord Pango came back from a hunting trip, saying he'd heard stories about dragons' eggs being seen somewhere."

"Eggs!" said the King, a light coming into his eyes. "Eggs. The very thing. Why didn't I think of it? Eggs. Eggs."

"What are you rambling on about now?, my love" asked the Queen. "You've surely heard of eggs before?"

"Yes, of course I have, but I didn't think of them as an answer to the dragon problem. I forgot that they take so long to hatch. Don't you see? If we can find a dragon's egg, we can bring it back here and hatch it out! So much easier than catching a young dragon in some wild spot, and bringing it home. An egg cannot run away or escape; it cannot bite or burn. A dragon's egg! We must find a dragon's egg. Quick, now, where did you say Pango heard of these eggs?"

"Oh . . . somewhere."

"I know it was *somewhere*, woman. Can't you be more exact than that? I can't tell my knights to go and search 'somewhere' for a dragon's egg, now can I?"

"Oh, I don't know," said the Queen vaguely; "it was in some wild place. Why don't you ask Pango himself! I wasn't listening properly when he talked of it. I was wondering if you could make an omelette with such an egg."

"Omelettes indeed!"shouted the King. "Just like a woman. Send for Lord Pango! Send him to me at once! I must have words with him."

Lord Pango was summoned. He had a long talk with the King, and there was much unrolling of maps, and deep considering over cup after cup of coffee, and the end of it was that Lord Pango set out a week later at the head of an expedition.

There was great excitement in the city when Lord

Pango set out. Cheering crowds lined the streets all the way to the North Gate. There were twenty knights in armour, with their squires, and a long baggage-train of mules, carrying all the tents and food and weapons needed for a long and dangerous journey into the wild, mountainous country to the north, far from the safety of the city walls. There

were fierce enemy tribes roaming the countryside, and Lord Pango and his men might have to stand and fight. Most important of all, they carried a magnificent casket, in which to carry the precious egg home. It rode in a beautiful palanquin, covered in cloth-of-gold and carried by four white horses, amid the glittering spears of the knights.

The last person to wave Lord Pango on his way was David, a boy who lived on a farm half-a-day's ride from the city. David's father kept hens and ducks and geese, and David helped with all the work of the farm. Once a week, he rode to market in the city, with two great baskets slung on his horse, full of eggs: small hens' eggs; larger duck eggs; still larger goose eggs. These he sold in the market. So he heard all the gossip of the people of the city and knew all about Lord Pango's expedition, for the city was all a-chatter about it.

"Godspeed! And a safe return!" he called after the knights. He gazed in wonder at the gold palanquin, and marvelled that such a costly thing should be made to carry a single egg.

Lord Pango and his knights travelled far. After many weary weeks, they found what they sought. On a wild peak of the Shivering Mountains, lodged behind a boulder, almost out of sight, was a real dragon's egg, creamy white and crimson veined. With trembling hands, they lifted it into the casket, wrapped it in soft silken cloths, and placed it gently in the golden palanquin. Then they made for home, with all speed. They were about half-way home when a roving band of Malandrian knights spotted the glinting of the sun upon their golden palanquin. The Malandrian knights hid by the track, in a narrow mountain pass, and laid an ambush. When Lord Pango and his men came past, the Malandrians fell upon them with fierce battle cries and took Lord Pango and all his proud knights prisoner without a fight, so great and sudden was their surprise. The dragon's egg was broken in the turmoil of the battle, and the Malandrians were greatly surprised when they looked inside the casket in the golden palanquin: expecting to find gold and jewels, they found only the mess of the broken egg. Malagorn, their leader, was very angry.

"What is this?" he shouted. "What is this mess? Where are your amethysts and sapphires? Where is your gold and silver? Come now. We know you

come to the mountains to seek treasure. Tell me where it is, or you die, every man of you."

Lord Pango fell on his knees before Malagorn.

"I beg you, my lord," he said, "not to kill us, for it

is against the laws of knighthood. Upon my honour as a knight, I swear to you that that *is* our treasure you see there. It is, or was, an egg."

"An egg? What madness is this? A band of knights out to seek an egg?"

"Yes, my lord. Our King, Calamy the First, has taken a sudden desire to have a certain very rare egg for his collection."

"What is its use?"

"It's use, sir? Why, sir, none that I know of. It is only that his collection is not complete without it."

"Your king sounds a fool to me, but I almost believe your silly story. However – no harm in searching you. Men! Search them! And if a single jewel is found, I will blunt my sword on your bones."

Every man was searched. Nothing was found. The Malandrians scowled in disappointment and climbed on their horses.

"To tell the truth," said Malagorn, "we need horses more than we need jewels. So we're taking yours. You'll have a long walk home. Farewell!"

Grinning now, they rode off, leaving Lord Pango and his men without a single horse among them.

For many days, Lord Pango's expedition trudged wearily across the wild countryside, each man laden with heavy armour, and tents, and the great sacks of food that the horses had carried. They were lucky enough not to be attacked again, but they were a sorry sight when they reached the North Gate of the city, five weeks later. Their clothes were in tatters and the golden palanquin was spattered all over with mud.

King Calamy was told of their arrival. When he saw them, he said, "What in the world have you been doing all this time? Just look at you! What have you done with your horses? Where's the dragon's egg? Quick, show it to me."

Silently, Lord Pango lifted the lid of the casket. The king saw a mass of broken shell, and a dreadful smell made him bang the lid down again.

"Is – was – that it?" he said.

"Yes," said Lord Pango sadly, and told the king the whole story.

"Well, what are we going to do now?" said King Calamy.

"Send another expedition," said the Queen.

So he did. The same thing happened again, but this time they were attacked by another war-band, who smashed their palanquin to pieces and stole the casket.

"It's the palanquin and casket that attracts the brigands," said the Queen. "Send an expedition without these things."

So King Calamy sent an expedition with a plain wooden box to collect the egg in, but they were attacked and put to flight before they even reached the mountains. By now, all the wandering bands of knights knew that King Calamy was trying to get a dragon's egg for hatching, for rumour and gossip had carried the news all over the land. They were determined to stop him, because they knew that a new dragon would be a great danger to them. King Calamy sent out more expeditions, but every one of them was attacked as soon as it was well clear of the safety of the city walls. Soon, it became dangerous for any soldier or knight to leave the city at all, and King Calamy despaired of ever getting a dragon's egg.

Then the Queen had another idea.

"Why not offer a prize to anyone who can bring a dragon's egg safely to the city?"

"Why not?" said the King. "It's our last chance. Our enemies will attack the city soon, if we don't get a new dragon. Yes, we'll do it."

So the heralds proclaimed a prize of one thousand gold pieces for anyone who brought a good dragon's egg safely to the King. This gave David an idea in his turn – David, the boy who brought his father's eggs to market: brown hens' eggs; big duck eggs; still bigger goose eggs.

One day, instead of riding to town with his big basket of eggs, he turned his horse toward the mountains. He carried simple provisions: bread and cheese, and a gourd of wine; and a small pan to cook eggs in. He soon met a roving band of knights, who were on the lookout for the king's expeditions.

"Who are you, and what is your business? What

have you got in those baskets?" demanded their leader.

"I am David. My father has a small farm, with hens, ducks, and geese. My baskets are full of eggs. I am on my way to the city beyond the mountains to sell my eggs, for I can get a better price there than in King Calamy's city. The people are poor there. All their money is spent in taxes to pay for fruitless expeditions."

The knight grinned at this, and said, "Go on your way, boy. We have no quarrel with honest traders, or with *duck* eggs."

And they let David go, unharmed. As he went on his way, he met many more bands of knights, and the same thing happened each time. When he reached the mountains, it was quieter, and he camped out many a night without seeing anyone. Then, he began to hunt for dragons' eggs. If he met anyone, he pretended simply to be travelling on toward the distant city, so that no one knew of his real quest. After many days of seeking, David was rewarded. He found a beautiful dragon egg, nestling under some broad ferns. It was marked all over with fine crimson lines – the one sure sign of a dragon egg, as he knew. He took some chalk dust from a

pouch on his belt and rubbed it all over the egg, making it white. Now it looked just like a goose egg, even if it was a little bit larger. He lifted a number of goose eggs out of one of his baskets, made a space, and gently placed the dragon egg in it. Then he covered it over with a good deep layer of goose eggs. He turned his horse round and headed back for home.

On the way back, David met many more bands of knights. Some looked suspiciously into his basket, but they all let him go on. It was quite obvious that he really was a seller of eggs, an innocent trader with no notions about dragons. David's worst moment was when he met a band of hungry knights, who were luckily honest and bought what they could easily have taken from him. They bought all his hen eggs, and all his duck eggs, and would have bought his goose eggs, too, but he said, "These eggs are for hatching, not eating, and so more costly. My father will beat me if I don't take them safely home; he hopes to hatch a great many geese for the Christmas fairs. Good, sir knights, please let me keep my goose eggs."

The knights laughed, and their leader said, "He shall keep his geese. Go on your way, boy: we'll not earn you a beating."

And so David came to the city gates at last, and went to the palace to tell King Calamy of his quest, and claim his reward.

"Is it possible?" said King Calamy, looking in

amazement at the basket of goose eggs. "Is it possible that a boy has succeeded where all my soldiers and brave knights have failed? Are you pulling my leg, boy? Come now, are you? It doesn't do to tease a king. I could have your head chopped off, just like that! You have dozens of eggs there."

"No, sire, it is true. I have brought you a dragon's egg. If you will send for a bowl of water, I will show you."

"Water? A bowl of water? The boy's crazy."

"Humour him," said the Queen. "Let's see what his game is."

Turning to a footman, she said, "Water. A bowl of water, at once."

The water was brought. David knelt before the king. He took his eggs from the basket, one by one. He washed each one carefully in the water and laid it on the grass. He could not guess himself, so good was the disguise, which was the dragon's egg; but he came at last to an egg that revealed a pattern of fine crimson lines when it was washed. He held it out to the king, in triumph.

"For you, your majesty. One dragon's egg. May I have my reward?"

"Indeed it is," whispered the King. "I have seen it just so, in my book of eggs. My boy, how did you do it, with the fields full of armed knights and brigands?"

"It was simple," said David. "I carry eggs to market every week. People are used to seeing me with baskets of eggs, so no one takes any notice when I pass by. When your knights march past with their glittering armour and bright flags, everyone notices, the word runs before them, and the enemy are on the lookout. No matter how your knights carried a dragon's egg, it would be found and destroyed. What better place to hide an egg than amongst a lot of other eggs?"

"No better place in all the world," laughed the King. "The boy has more brains that the rest of us put together. Give him the thousand gold pieces. He's earned them."

David returned home rich and famous. The egg was hatched, and a fine new dragon came out of it, and King Calamy's city was safe for another nine hundred years.

THE DRAGON AND THE MONKEY

A Chinese Tale

Far away in the China Seas lived a dragon and his wife. She was fretful and rather difficult, but he was a kind and loving dragon. As they swam in the warm seas together she was forever complaining and asking her husband to fetch her different foods. He always thought, "This time I will really make her happy, and then how easy and lovely life will be." Yet somehow, whatever delicacy he fetched her, she was never satisfied and always wanted something else.

One day she twitched her tail more than usual, and told her husband that she was not feeling well and that she had heard a monkey's heart was the only thing to cure her.

"You are certainly looking ill," said the dragon, "and you know I would do anything for you, but how can I possibly find you a monkey's heart? Monkeys live up trees, and I could never catch one."

"Now I know you don't love me," cried his wife. "If you did you would find a way to catch one. Now I shall surely die!"

The dragon sighed and swam off across the seas to an island where he knew some monkeys lived. "Somehow," he thought desperately, "I must trick a monkey into coming with me, for I cannot let my wife die."

When he reached the island, he saw a little monkey sitting in a tree. The dragon called out, "Hello, monkey! It's good to see you! Come down and talk to me. That tree looks so unsafe, you might fall out!"

At that the monkey roared with laughter. "Ha! Ha! Ha! You are funny, dragon. Whoever heard of a monkey falling out of a tree?"

The dragon thought of his wife and tried again.

"I'll show you a tree covered with delicious juicy fruit, monkey. It grows on the other side of the sea."

Again the monkey laughed. "Ha! Ha! Ha! Whoever heard of a monkey swimming across the sea, dragon?"

"I could take you on my back, little monkey," said the dragon.

The monkey liked this idea and swung out of the tree onto the dragon's back. As he swam across the sea, the dragon thought there was no way the monkey could escape, so he said, "There are no trees with delicious fruit where we are going. I am taking you to my wife who wishes to have your heart. She says it is the only thing that will cure her of her illness."

The monkey looked at the water all around him and saw no way to escape, but he thought quickly, and said, "Your poor wife! I am sorry to hear she's not well. There is nothing I'd like more than to give her my heart. But what a pity you did not tell me before we left. You obviously did not know, dragon, that we monkeys never carry our hearts with us. I left it behind in the tree where you found me. If you would be kind enough to swim back there with me, I shall willingly fetch it."

So the dragon turned around and swam back to the place where he had found the monkey. With one leap the monkey was in the branches of the tree, safe out of the dragon's reach.

"I'm sorry to disappoint you, dragon," he called out, "but I had my heart with me all the time. You won't trick me out of this tree again. Ha! Ha! Ha!"

There was no way the dragon could reach him and whether or not he ever caught another monkey I do not know. Perhaps he is still looking while his wife swims alone in the China Seas.

For permission to reproduce copyright material
acknowledgement and thanks are due to the following:

Little, Brown & Co. for "Assipattle and the Giant Sea
Serpent" from *Favorite Fairy Tales Told in Scotland* by
Virginia Haviland. Text copyright ©1963 by Virginia
Haviland. J. M. Dent and Sons Ltd for "Frightening the
Monster in Wizard's Hole" from *Nonstop Nonsense* by
Margaret Mahy, copyright © 1977 by Margaret Mahy.
Jonathan Cape Ltd for "The Giant Who Threw
Tantrums" from *The Book of Giant Stories* copyright ©
David L. Harrison 1972. Reprinted by permission of the
author. Scholastic Publications Ltd. for "King Calamy
and the Dragon's Egg" from *The Great Dragon
Competition and Other Stories* by John Cunliffe (1976).

Stories retold from traditional sources that in this
version are © Grisewood & Dempsey are as follows:
"Thor's Stolen Hammer" (1991) and "The Little Bull
Calf" (1991) are retold by Eugenie Summerfield. "The
Giant's Clever Wife," (1988), "Jack and the Beanstalk"
(1988), and "Beauty and the Beast" (1988) are retold by
Nora Clarke. "The Giant with the Three Golden Hairs"
(1989) is retold by Marie Greenwood. "The Dragon and
the Monkey" (1982) is retold by Linda Yeatman.

Every effort has been made to obtain permission from
copyright holders. If, regrettably, any omissions have
been made, we shall be pleased to make suitable
corrections in any reprint.

Titles in the
Kingfisher Treasury series

~